A
CIRCLE
OF
SEASONS

Myra Cohn Livingston

POET

Leonard Everett Fisher

PAINTER

Holiday House / New York

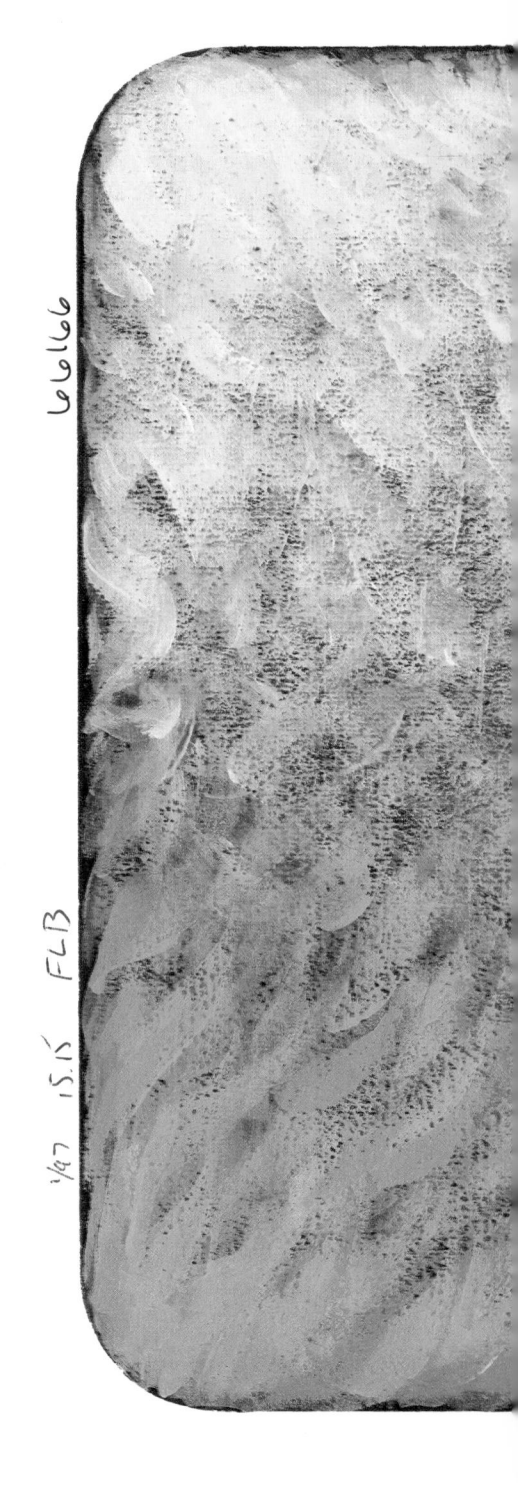

Text copyright © 1982 by Myra Cohn Livingston
Illustrations copyright © 1982 by Leonard Everett Fisher
All rights reserved
Printed in the United States of America

Library of Congress Cataloging in Publication Data

Livingston, Myra Cohn.
A circle of seasons.

Summary: A thirteen-stanza poem following the cycle
of the seasons.
1. Children's poetry, American.   2. Seasons—Juvenile
poetry. [1. Seasons—Poetry. 2. American poetry]
I. Fisher, Leonard Everett, ill.   II. Title.
PS3562.I945C5   811'.54   81-20305
ISBN 0-8234-0452-8   AACR2
ISBN 0-8234-0656-3 (pbk.)

Spring skips lightly on a thin crust of snow,
Pokes her fragrant fingers in the ground far below,
Searches for the sleeping seeds hiding in cracked earth,
Sticks a straw of sunshine down and whispers words to grow:

O seed
And root,
Send forth a tiny shoot!

Spring brings out her baseball bat, swings it through the air,
Pitches bulbs and apple blossoms, throws them where it's bare,
Catches dogtooth violets, slides to meadowsweet,
Bunts a breeze and tags the trees with green buds everywhere.

O April,
March and May,
Come watch us at our play!

Spring pipes at the peeper frogs, mocks the mockingbird,
Hears a ring of harebells, a mourning dove's soft word,
Bubbles with stream waters, splatters with warm rain,
Listens to the rustling a wakening breeze has stirred.

O laugh
And sing,
Give welcome to the Spring!

Summer blasts off fireworks, fuses them with red,
Sets them off to sizzle in a star-sky overhead,
Bursts them into color as they shower back to earth,
Steams them up with sunshine in a blazing flower bed.

O sun,
Shine higher,
Heat us with your fire!

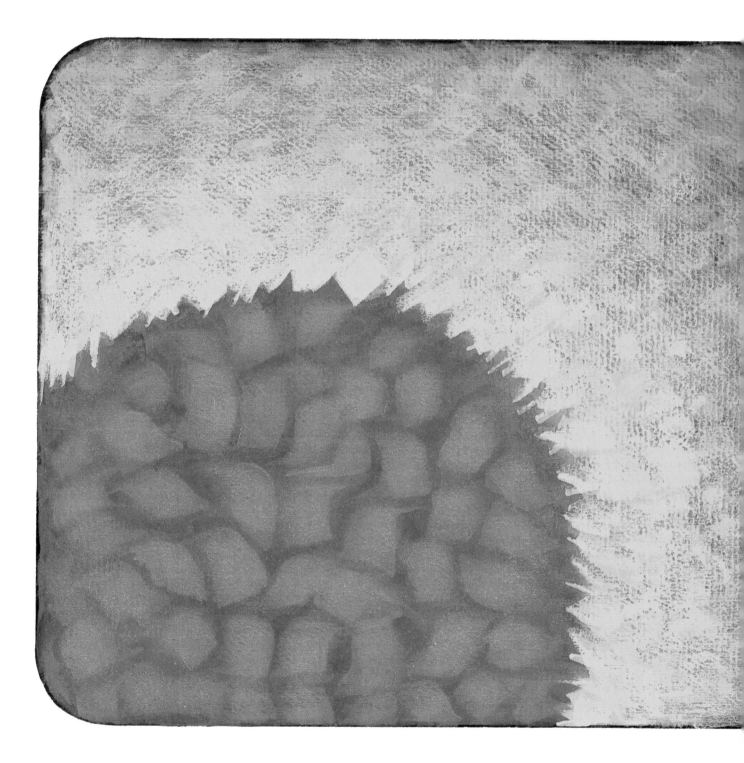

Summer wades the waters where distant islands gleam,
Skims across the whitecaps, pulls mermaids from a stream,
Fishes for a frog prince, dives deep for hidden gold,
Drifts in a sea of castle-clouds and flows into a dream.

O water,
Clear and blue,
Make one small wish come true!

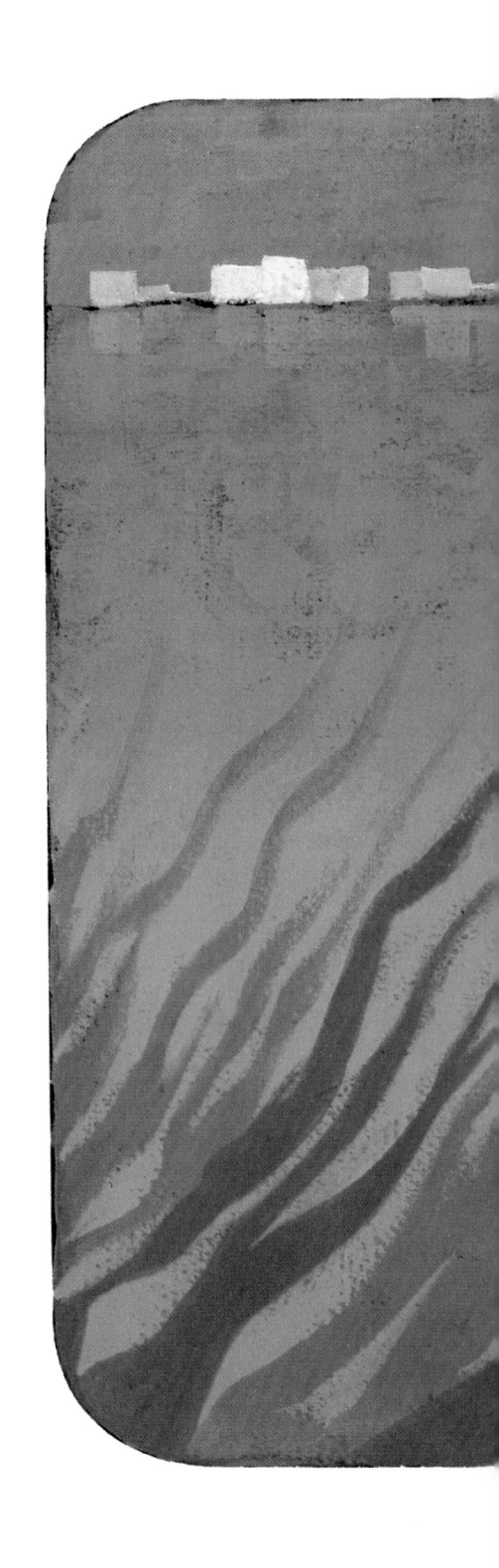

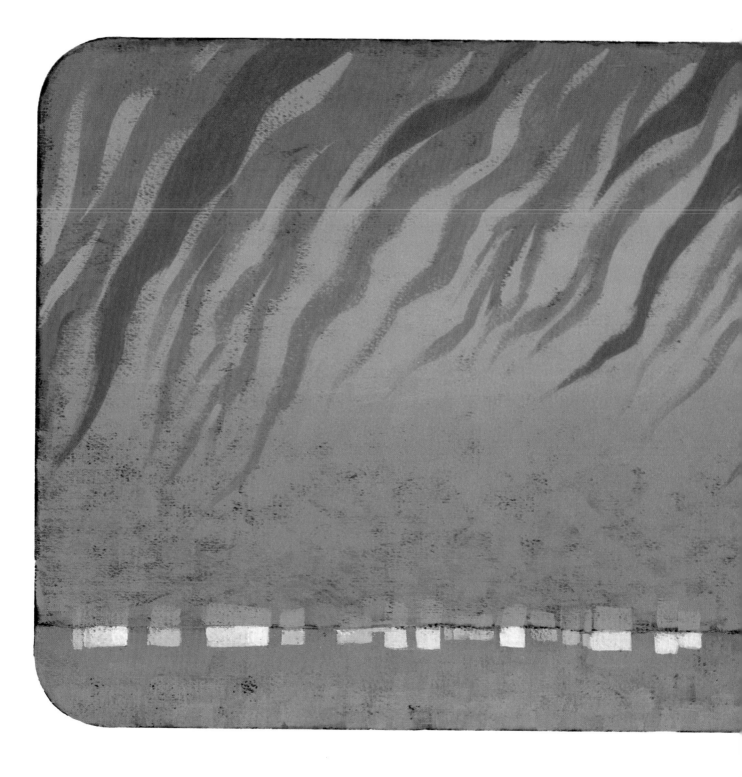

Summer fattens melons up, grows berries plump and sweet,
Wraps corn in sheaths of tassled silk, shucks them out to eat,
Stains her lips with cherry juice, bites purple plum and peach,
Sucks sticky juice from featherweed, pours gold on fields of wheat.

O vine
And field,
We gather in your yield!

Autumn scuffs across the earth, leaves it patched and brown,
Holds his cap to catch the acorns falling to the ground,
Watches as the wild geese wheel up their landing gear,
Sees a nipping wind whirl red and yellow leaf around.

O leaves,
Fly near
This lonely time of year!

Autumn calls the winning toss, passes for a gain,
Blocks the frost with bittersweet, tackles pouring rain,
Intercepts with smoky haze, makes a last long play,
Scores as Winter's whistle blows, touches down in vain.

O world,
Stand tall
Against the back of Fall!

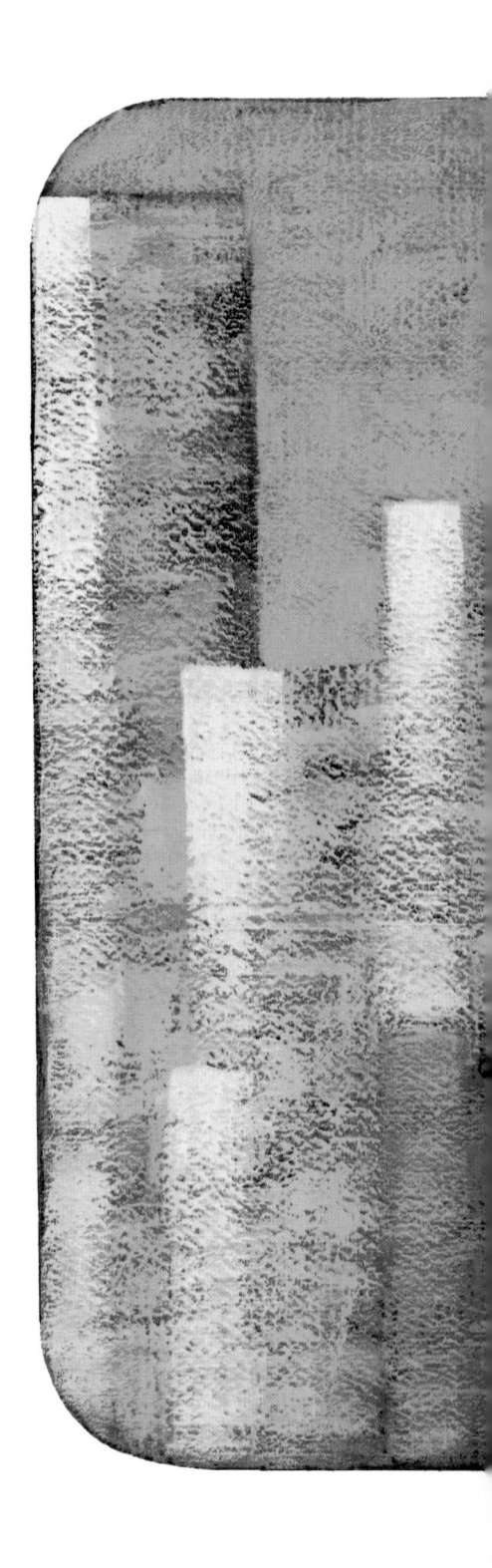

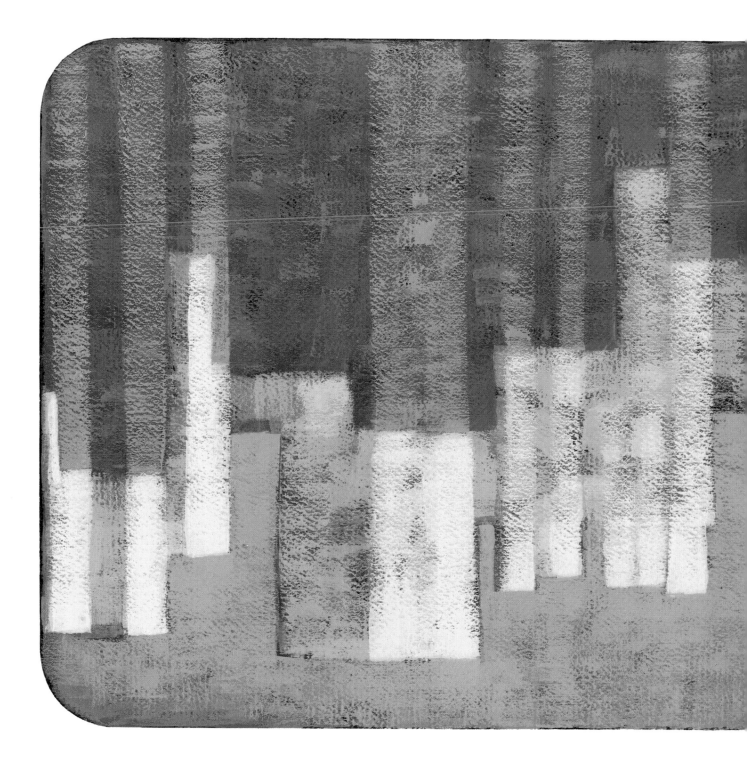

Autumn leaves a fringe of frost when pumpkins turn to gold,
Pulls his collar up to warm his face grown gray and old,
Gathers in his harvest, says a prayer of thanks,
Gives a little shiver, and all the air turns cold.

O earth,
Rest well
Under the Autumn spell!

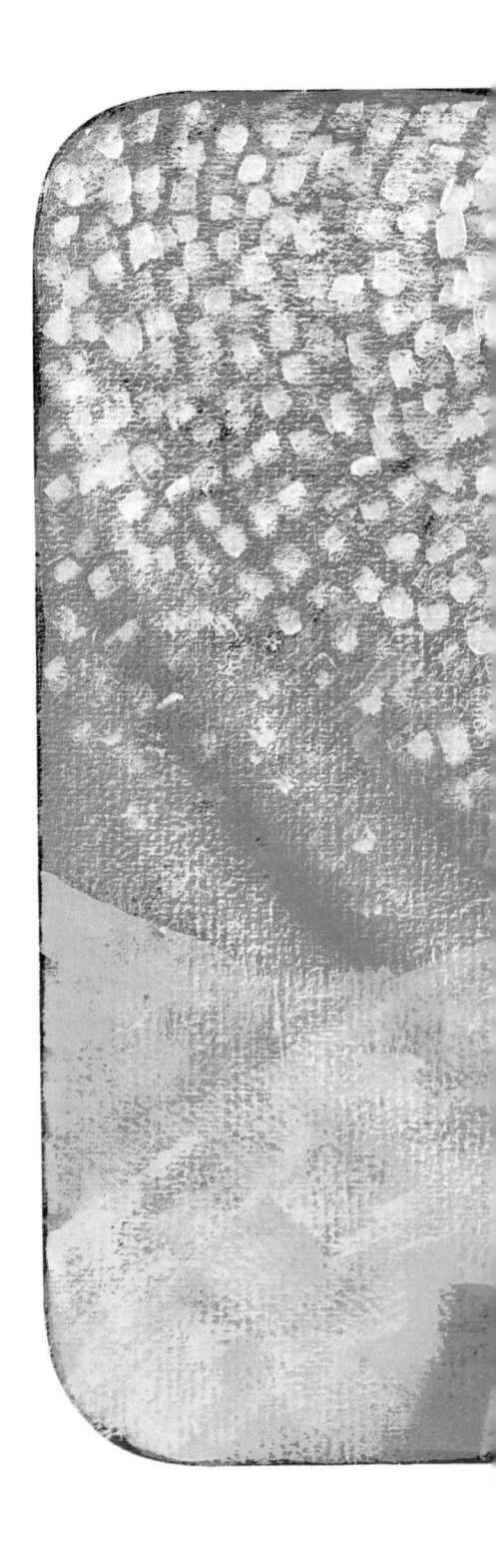

Winter blows a blizzard, rages with a gale,
Spews ice crystals through the clouds, pellets earth with hail,
Breathes a freezing snowstorm, buries hedge and path,
Quiets down in chalky drifts, on mornings bleak and pale.

O world,
Lie still
Beneath the biting chill!

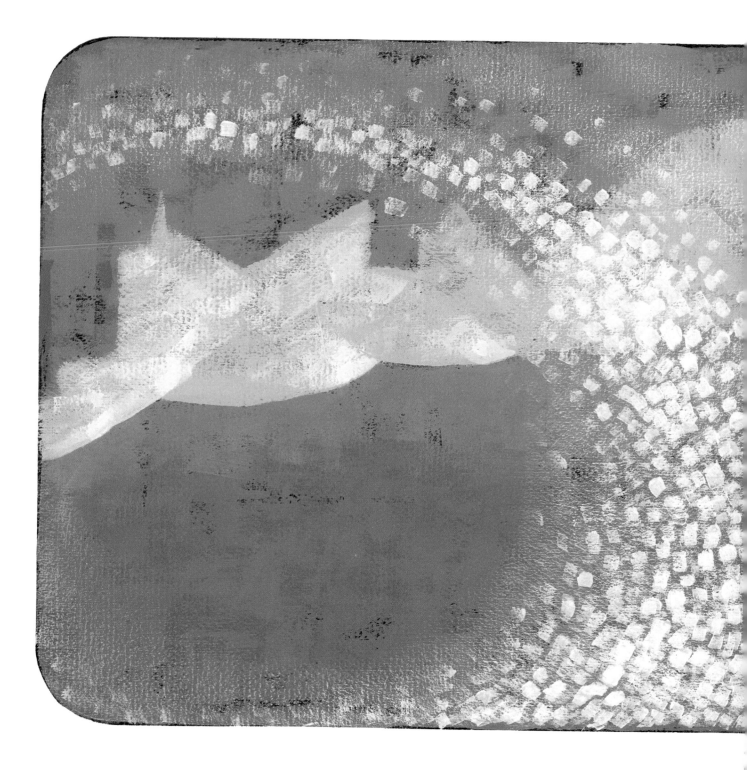

Winter etches windowpanes, fingerpaints in white,
Sculptures strange soft shapes of snow that glister in the night,
Filigrees the snowflake, spins icicles of glass,
Paints the ground in hoarfrost, its needles sharp with light.

O bush
And pine,
You, too, shall brightly shine!

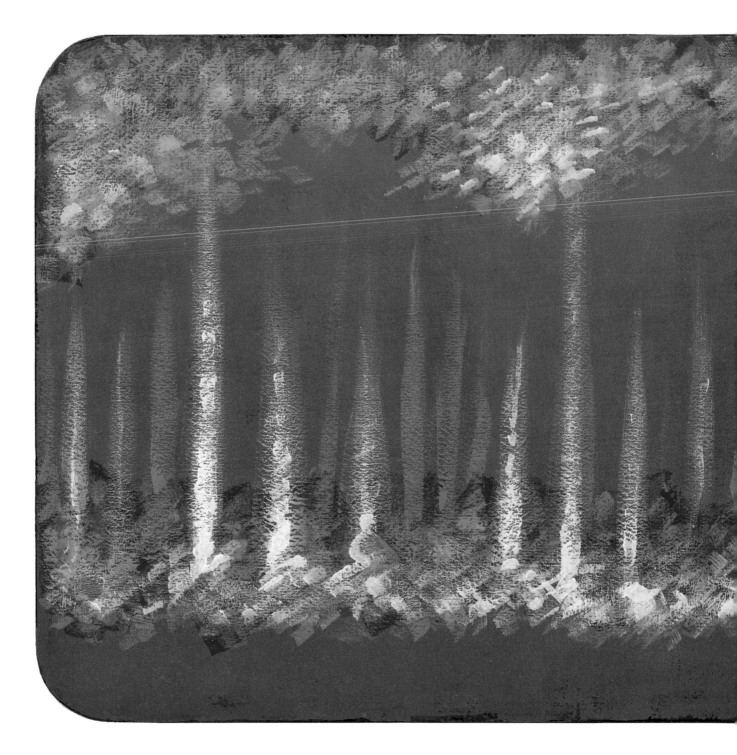

Winter wakes to changing wind, gives a little cry,
Sees a fluttering of wings, a blue jay darting by,
The greening of skunk cabbage, a warm breeze stirring air,
The thinning snow crust and above—a blue patch in the sky.

O Winter,
Weep,
The earth's no more asleep!

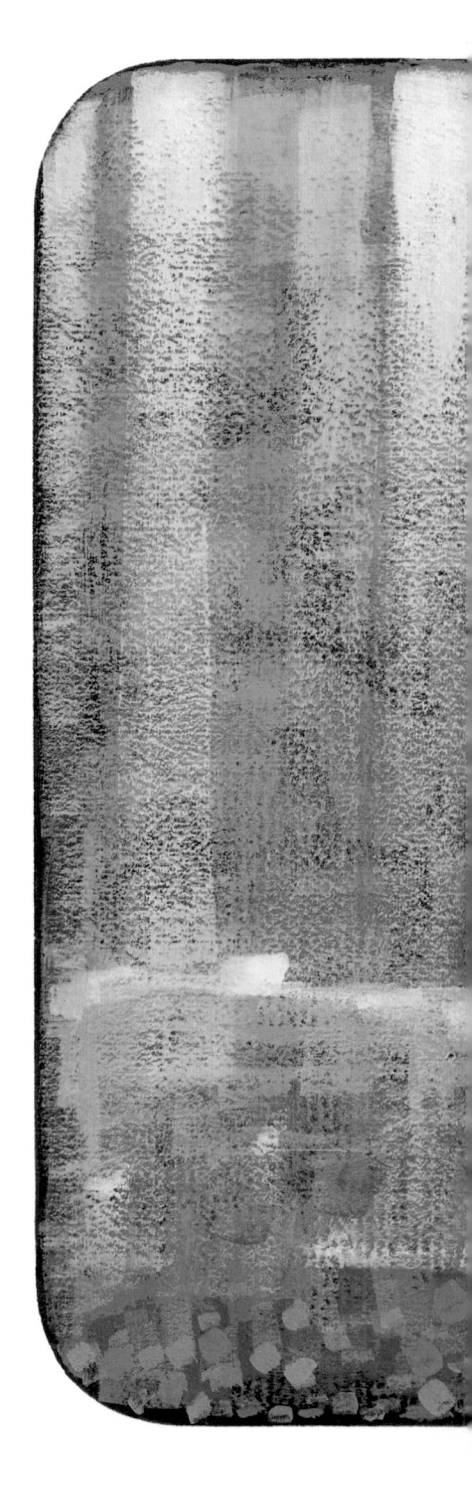

Spring skips lightly on a thin crust of snow,
Pokes her fragrant fingers in the ground far below,
Searches for the sleeping seeds hiding in cracked earth,
Sticks a straw of sunshine down and whispers words to grow:

O life,
O birth,
You start again in earth!